**PENNY MCKINLAY** began her career as a newspaper journalist, before moving into. television news. She has also written *Flabby Tabby*, illustrated by Britta Teckentrup.

**BRITTA TECKENTRUP** is a graduate of the Royal College of Art. Britta's first book was described by *Publishers Weekly* as *"magic"*, and she hasn't looked back since. Author and illustrator of more than 60 children's books published in over 20 countries, her work is elegant and child-like at the same time. Britta lives in Berlin with her husband and son.

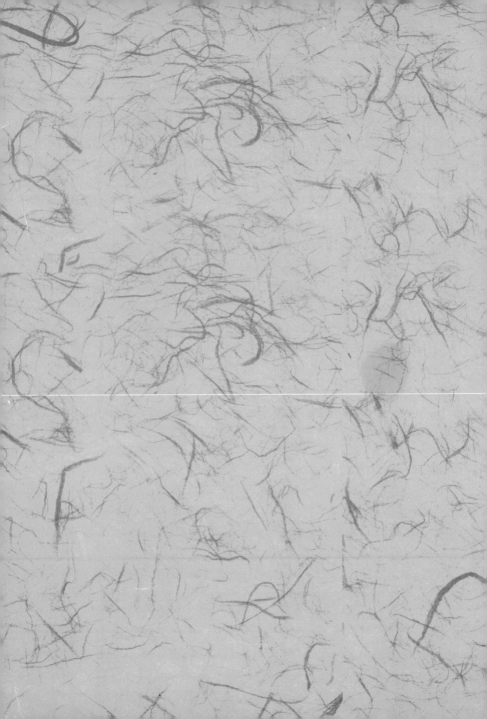

To Holly who helped, and to Scott - P.M.
To Vincent, our beautiful baby boy - B.T.

Text © Penny McKinlay 2003, 2014
Illustrations © Britta Teckentrup 2003, 2014

The rights of Penny McKinlay and Britta Teckentrup to be identified
respectively as the author and illustrator of this Work have been asserted by
them in accordance with the Copyright, Designs and Patent Act, 1988.

First published in Great Britain in 2003.
This early reader edition published in Great Britain and in the USA
in 2014 by Frances Lincoln Children's Books,
74-77 White Lion Street, London, N1 9PF
www.franceslincoln.com

A CIP catalogue record for this book is available from the British Library.

ISBN 978-184780-542-3

Printed in China

1 3 5 7 9 8 6 4 2

# BUMPOSAURUS

**Penny McKinlay**
**Illustrated by Britta Teckentrup**

**F**

FRANCES LINCOLN
CHILDREN'S BOOKS

There once was a baby dinosaur who was so short-sighted he couldn't find his way out of his egg. Bump! Bump! Bump! he went inside his shell.

His mother heard him bumping and helped him out.
"I think we'll call you Bumposaurus!" she said.

Bumposaurus ran off past his brothers and sisters.

He ran over the edge of the sandy hollow.

He fell down a very steep hill.

And he landed in a very deep bog.

"Mummy!" called the other baby dinosaurs.
"Bumpy is stuck!"
Mother hauled him out. She licked the mud off his
nose. "He likes adventure!" she said to Daddy.

"Come and play chase, Bumpy!" cried his brothers
and sisters. "You're it!" And they ran off giggling.
Bumposaurus stretched his long neck. He looked this
way and that. "Where are you?" he called.
"We are over here!" they cried. They creeped closer.

He still could not see them.
"Here!" they cried. They creeped even closer.
"There you are!" cried Bumposaurus.
He swung round and knocked them down.
Bump! Bump! Bump!

Mummy gave them each a loving lick. "Lunch-time!"
she said.
Lunch was leaves. Lunch was always leaves.
"Not leaves again," moaned the babies.
"Now children," said Daddy. "You know we do not eat
other dinosaurs!"

Bumposaurus began to munch. But it turned out to
be his sister's tail.
"Daddy!" she yelled. "Bumpy is eating me!"
"Bumposaurus!" said Daddy. "Eating dinosaurs
is wrong!"

After lunch, Bumposaurus went off to explore. Bump!
He hit his head. He looked up. He saw something
above him.
"Daddy, I am sorry," he said. I didn't see you."
Daddy said nothing.

"I did not mean to eat Bella."
Still Daddy said nothing.
"Daddy, I think there's something wrong with me.
I am different from the others."
And he told his story.

But Daddy still said nothing. He could not because it
was not Daddy.
It was a tree!

"I am going to leave home if you are angry,"
said Bumposaurus. And he set off.
Bumposaurus came to the edge of a wide river.
"These logs will stop my feet getting wet."

"What a hot day it is!"

"Where is everybody?"

By now Bumposaurs felt like giving up and going
home. He was covered in bumps. He was tired
and lonely.

He longed for a lick from Mummy.
He fell into a sandy hollow.
"I am home!" he cried. And he fell asleep.

The T rex was sleeping off a meal. He had definitely not been eating leaves! He was very surprised when he woke to find a small Brontosaurus fast asleep in his nest.

"Yum!" he said. He gave Bumpy a lick.

"You're not my mummy," yelped Bumpy, waking up with
a jump.

And the T rex grinned a horrible grin with sharp teeth.

But just at that moment there came a thundering sound of forty stomping feet. Ten angry Brontosaurus faces looked down into the hollow.

"Put my son down!" Daddy shouted. "Eating dinosaurs is wrong!"
The T rex said, "Quite right, quite right. What was I thinking of? Sorry!" And he ran off.

When Bumposaurus got home, his mummy gave
him the most loving lick ever. "Say hello to Grandma,
Bumposaurus," she said.
"Where?" said Bumposaurus.
"Here."

A soft face bent close to his face. "Now you can see me, can't you?" she said.

"What are those circles round your eyes, Grandma?" asked Bumpy.

"Try them on, and see, little one," she said.

Bumposaurus slid the glasses on to his nose.
At once he saw smiling faces looking at him.

At last he could see!

# Collect the TIME TO READ books:

978-1-84780-476-1

978-1-84780-475-4

978-1-84780-477-8

978-1-84780-478-5

978-1-84780-543-0

978-1-84780-544-7

978-1-84780-542-3

978-1-84780-545-4

Frances Lincoln titles are available from all good bookshops.
You can also buy books and find out more about your favourite titles,
authors and illustrators on our website: www.franceslincoln.com